Emmy
the Exaggerating
Elephant

Fenton
the Fearful Frog

Gertie
the Grungy Goat

the Happy
Hamster

the Impatient
Iguana

Ollie
the Obedient
Ostrich

Perry
the Polite
Porcupine

Queenie
the Quiet Quail

Rupert
the Resourceful
Rhinoceros

Ziggy
the Zippy Zebra

Wendy
the Wise
Woodchuck

Xavier
the X-ploring
Xenops

Yori
the Yucky Yak

NOTE TO PARENTS

Fenton and the Magic Bag
A story about self-confidence

In this story, Fenton the Fearful Frog is so worried and afraid of trying new things that it keeps him from enjoying the Fall Fun Festival. Thanks to his AlphaPet friends, Fenton meets Fernando the Fabulous Fortune Teller who thinks of a magic way to show Fenton how to believe in himself and be brave.

In addition to enjoying this touching story with your child, you can use it to teach a gentle lesson about the important value of self-confidence — believing in yourself to overcome fears, worries and obstacles.

You can also use this story to introduce the letter **F**. As you read about Fenton the Fearful Frog, ask your child to listen for all the **F** words and point to the objects that begin with **F**. When you've finished reading the story, your child will enjoy doing the activity at the end of the book.

The AlphaPets™ characters were conceived and created by Ruth Lerner Perle.
Characters interpreted and designed by Deborah Colvin Borgo.
Cover design by the Antler & Baldwin Design Group.
Book design and production by Publishers' Graphics, Inc.
Logo design by Deborah Colvin Borgo and Nancy S. Norton.

Printed and Manufactured in the United States of America

Fenton and the Magic Bag

RUTH LERNER PERLE

Illustrated by Judy Blankenship

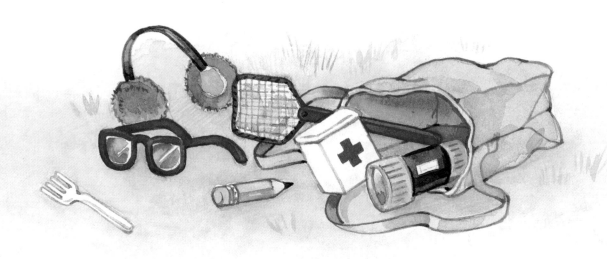

Grolier Enterprises Inc.   Danbury, Connecticut

Fenton the Fearful Frog was getting ready to go to the Fall Fun Festival with his AlphaPet friends.

"Before I leave home, I'd better make sure I have everything I need — just in case," said Fenton. "Let's see, I have bandages in case I fall and hurt my ankle.

I have iodine in case I scrape my knee. I have a sweater in case it gets too cold and a fan in case it gets too hot. I need a map in case I get lost, and snacks in case I get hungry. Here's my umbrella in case it rains and my sunglasses in case it's too sunny."

Fenton stuffed everything into his bag. Then he added a hot water bottle, five hankies, a sewing kit, a flashlight, earmuffs, safety pins, forks, spoons, a fly swatter, and a small fire extinguisher.

FALL FUN
FESTIVAL
Fernando
FOOT RACE
4:00

Soon the AlphaPets came to pick up Fenton.

Tina the Truthful Tiger looked at Fenton's bulging bag.

"If you have to carry all that, you won't be able to run and jump and play," she said.

"How will you enjoy the Snake Slide, the Bumper Cars, and the Rocket Roller Coaster?" asked Xavier the X-ploring Xenops.

"Snake Slide? Bumper Cars? Roller Coaster?" asked Fenton.

"Of course," added Ollie the Obedient Ostrich. "And the main event will be a fantastic Free-For-All Foot Race.

"Oh no!" cried Fenton, and he started to shiver and shake. "I'll never be able to do all that. You'd better go without me."

"Oh, Fenton," said Wendy the Wise Woodchuck. "Anything we can do, you can do, too. Trust yourself and stop worrying. You'll have a wonderful time."

"Especially if you follow all the rules," said Ollie.

The AlphaPets took Fenton by the hand, and together they walked to the fairground.

The Fall Fun Festival looked just like a fantastic fairyland. There were flags flying, flowers blooming, all kinds of rides and floats, and a giant food pavillion.

The AlphaPets bought their tickets and went inside.

"Let's get in line for the Snake Slide," cried Xavier.

Fenton looked up toward the top of the slide. "Ooh," he whispered. "That slide is so high. I don't think I'll be able to climb those steep steps. I know I won't like it, and maybe it's not safe."

"It's safe if you follow all the safety instructions," said Ollie. "See, the sign shows that you're just the right size for the ride."

But Fenton stepped out of the line and watched while the others took turns sliding down.

The next ride was the Rocket Roller Coaster, but Fenton didn't go on that either.

"I'm afraid of fast rides," said Fenton. "I might get sick or dizzy."

And when they went to ride the Bumper Cars, Fenton said, "I'm afraid I won't know how to steer. What if I have an accident and fall out?"

"If you don't like the rides," said Tina, "let's go to the Batting Box. You'll get a prize if you hit the ball."

"Not me," said Fenton. "I'm not a good batter. And what if I miss the ball and it hits me?"

"Then let's go boating," said Ollie.

"I'm not strong enough to row," answered Fenton. "And what if the boat tips and I fall in the water?"

"OK, then let's sign up for the Free-For-All Foot Race," suggested Xavier. "It starts at four o'clock, and it's sure to be lots of fun."

"But what if I trip and fall and scrape my knee?" Fenton asked.

START

"I have an idea," Wendy said. "Let's go see Fernando the Fabulous Fortune Teller. He can tell the future and he does fantastic magic tricks."

"I guess I could go with you," said Fenton. "I hope it isn't too dark in there."

They went into Fernando's booth.

"*Velcome, Velcome,* my friends," said Fernando, standing behind his camera. "I must take *zee* picture to study *zee* faces," he said. "*Zay* cheese, *pleeze.*"

Fernando snapped the camera and disappeared behind a velvet curtain. "*Vait* here, *pleeze.*"

When Fernando called them, the AlphaPets followed him behind the curtain.

"Aha!" said Fernando, looking into a big crystal ball. "I *zee zat zomeone* in *zees* room *eez* carrying a VERY heavy burden."

"That must be Fenton," said Tina. "He's carrying a big bag in case something goes wrong."

"*Heez* burden *eez* greater than *heez* bag," said Fernando. "*Heez* burden *eez* fear and lack of confidence. But *zee* great Fernando *vill* fix *zat*."

Fernando pointed his finger at Fenton.

"Today *eez* your lucky day, my fine friend," he said, twirling his mustache. He pulled out a small felt pouch and gave it to Fenton.

"Wh . . . wh . . . what's this?" asked Fenton.

"*Zees* little bag has *zee* powerful magic inside it," said Fernando. "As long as you carry it, you *vill* not be afraid. It has all *zat* you *vill* ever need to succeed."

"Are you sure?" asked Fenton.

"Very sure. Trust me, and you *vill zee*," said Fernando.

"*Pleeze* leave your big old bag here," continued Fernando. "Go out and enjoy *zee* rides and *zee* games. No harm *vill* come to you. *Zee* magic in *zee* bag *vill* protect you."

Fernando put a tiny lock on the little bag.

"*Vee* must be sure to keep *zee* magic safe," he said. "Come back here when you are ready to go home. *Vee vill* unlock *zee* bag and you *vill zee* for yourself what *zee* magic is."

When the AlphaPets left Fernando's booth, Fenton followed his friends to the Snake Slide. He looked up toward the top of the slide. The steps seemed high, but not as high as before.

"Maybe, just maybe, I can do it," Fenton said to himself. Slowly, he climbed up. When he was almost at the top, his foot slipped on one step, but Fenton held on to the handrail and he didn't fall.

"That sure is powerful magic in my bag," thought Fenton as he stood at the top of the slide.

Fenton went over to the Rocket Roller Coaster. He sat down in a car next to Xavier.

"Courage," said Xavier. He put his arm around Fenton's shoulder.

When the roller coaster went swooping up, Fenton's stomach felt a little queasy. But he thought of the magic power he was carrying with him, and he sat tight. After a while he even enjoyed himself!

Then, Fenton went to the Batting Box. He took a bat, and waited for the ball to come his way.

Swoosh! Fenton missed the first ball.

Swoosh! He missed the next ball.

Then, *Crack!* Fenton hit the ball and won a prize!

It was four o'clock, and time for the foot race. All the racers were getting ready.

"Let's enter the race," called Ollie.

"I'm not a very good runner," said Fenton, "but I'll do my best. As long as I have my magic bag, I know I'll be safe."

Fenton got his number, and walked over to the starting line. When the whistle blew, he ran and ran and ran as hard as he could. He saw Ziggy the Zippy Zebra and Ivy the Impatient Iguana and some other AlphaPets pass him by, but he kept on running. Fenton's heart was beating and his legs were getting tired, but he did not give up until he reached the finish line.

"Hooray! Good for you, Fenton!" cried all the racing fans. "You made it! You didn't win, but you did your best."

"I feel terrific!" said Fenton.

"That sure is a powerful magic bag," said Fenton. "Look at all the things I can do without hurting myself. I think I'm ready for the Bumper Cars and then the rowboats."

Ollie looked at his watch. "It's almost five o'clock," he said. "The fair will be closing soon. We'd better get back to Fernando's booth so we can unlock the bag and see what the magic is."

Fernando was waiting in his booth.

"We've come to see what's in the magic bag. It must be all-powerful," said Fenton.

"But it *eez* all powerful," said Fernando. "You can *always* depend on it."

Fernando gave a little golden key to Fenton.

"You *vill pleeze* unlock *zee* bag now," he said.

Everyone watched as Fenton opened the bag. He reached in and pulled out an envelope with a picture inside it. Fenton looked at the picture.

"But —, but — I don't understand!" cried Fenton. "This is just a picture of *me*! Where is the special magic power?"

"It *is* you, Fenton," said Fernando, taking off his disguise. "The secret all-powerful magic ingredient is *you*! If you believe in yourself, there is *nothing* you can't do."

"I guess so," said Fenton, with a little smile.

"I guess *so*!"

The AlphaPets clapped and hugged their friend. They cried, "Good for you, Fenton, you not-so-fearful frog!"

Don't be afraid to learn these fabulous words with me.

fence

fan

fork

fish

4 four

flowers

5 five

flag

fire extinguisher

flashlight

Look back at the pictures in this book and try to find these and other things that begin with the letter F.

Know Your Alphabet

Aa Bb

Gg Hh

Mm Nn Oo Pp

Uu Vv Ww